Little Rabbit and the Night Mare

Written by   Illustrated by

Kate Klise   M. Sarah Klise

Harcourt, Inc.   *Orlando   Austin   New York   San Diego   London*

www.HarcourtBooks.com

Library of Congress Cataloging-in-Publication Data
Klise, Kate.
Little Rabbit and the night mare/Kate Klise;
illustrated by M. Sarah Klise.
p. cm.
Summary: Little Rabbit is so worried about his first school
report that his sleep is troubled by a terrifying night mare.
[1. Nightmares—Fiction. 2. Schools—Fiction. 3. Worry—Fiction.
4. Rabbits—Fiction.] I. Klise, M. Sarah, ill. II. Title.
PZ7.K684Lit 2008
[E]—dc22   2006038233
ISBN 978-0-15-205717-6

First edition
A C E G H F D B

Printed in Singapore

The illustrations in this book were done in acrylic on Bristol board.
The display type was created by M. Sarah Klise.
The text type was set in Brioso.
Color separations by Colourscan Co. Pte. Ltd., Singapore
Printed and bound by Tien Wah Press, Singapore
Production supervision by Christine Witnik
Designed by April Ward

For baby Lionel

It started on Monday, when
Little Rabbit's teacher gave the class an assignment.

"I want you each to prepare a report on the topic of your choice," she said. "You will present your report in front of the whole class on Friday."

On the walk home from school, Little Rabbit told his mother about the assignment.

"I need to think of a good topic," said Little Rabbit.

"Oh, there are lots of good topics," Mother Rabbit replied. "You could give your report about bugs or clouds."

But Little Rabbit didn't like those topics.

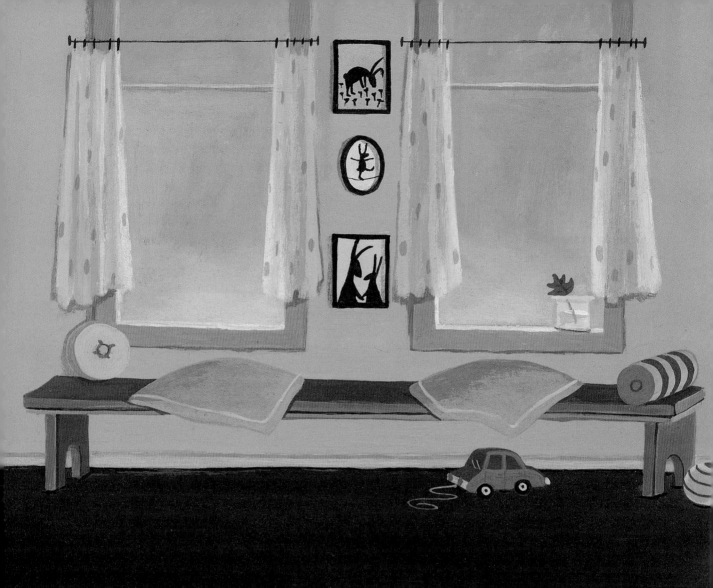

"What about carrots or airplanes or the moon?"
Mother Rabbit suggested during dinner. "Or reindeer?
Hummingbirds? Stars?"

Little Rabbit didn't like those topics, either. "This is
my first report," he said. "It has to be wonderful. I must

And Little Rabbit began to worry

That night, when Little Rabbit was sleeping
and worrying about his report, something
strange happened.

A mysterious creature appeared in his
dream and carried him away.

The beast flew so fast, Little Rabbit could
not hold on. He fell off and screamed.

"What is it?" Mother Rabbit asked.

"I don't know," Little Rabbit said breathlessly. "It was something terrible. I was flying on it, and then I fell."

Mother Rabbit rubbed his foot. "That was a nightmare," she said softly.

"A *night mare*?" asked Little Rabbit.

"Yes." said his mother. "But it's gone now. Everything's all right. Go back to sleep."

But Little Rabbit couldn't sleep.
He stayed up all night, worrying the
night mare would return.

The next day at school, Little Rabbit was still worried.

While his friends worked on their reports,
Little Rabbit was thinking about the night mare.

On Tuesday night, Little Rabbit made a sign
for his window. And then he made another
sign for his bed. And another for his wall.

But the night mare returned. For hours,
it flew fast and recklessly. The horrible horse

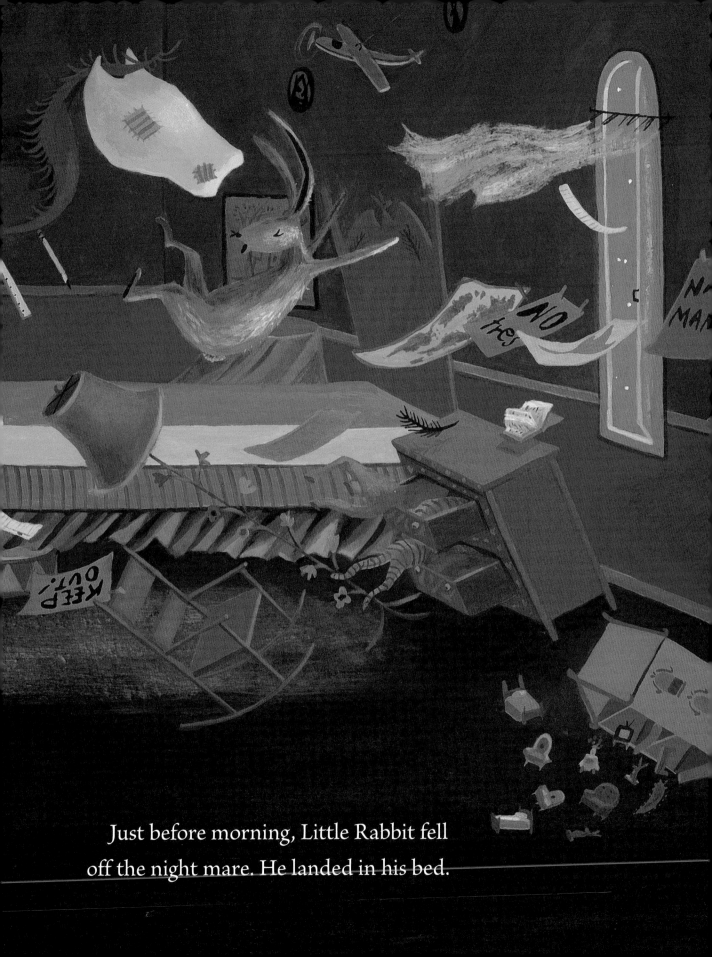

Just before morning, Little Rabbit fell
off the night mare. He landed in his bed.

"I hate the night mare," Little Rabbit grumbled
on Wednesday morning.

"I know you do," Mother Rabbit said. "But it won't
hurt you. I know that nightmare."

"Then make it stay away!" Little Rabbit demanded.

"I'm sorry, but I can't," Mother Rabbit said gently. "It's *your* nightmare. You must look it in the eye, and tell it to stop bothering you."

"How can I look it in the eye?!" cried Little Rabbit. "It's too scary. I wish the night mare would leave me alone so I could work on my report. I don't even have

Little Rabbit spent Wednesday afternoon
building a trap for the night mare. He gathered
his umbrella and a broom and a big net. He used

Then he assembled the trap in his bedroom and waited.

He waited.

And waited.

But the mare didn't visit that night.

By Thursday, Little Rabbit was exhausted.

He was too tired to work on his report.

All he could do was think about the night mare . . .

worry about the night mare . . .

daydream about
the night mare . . .

watch for the night mare.

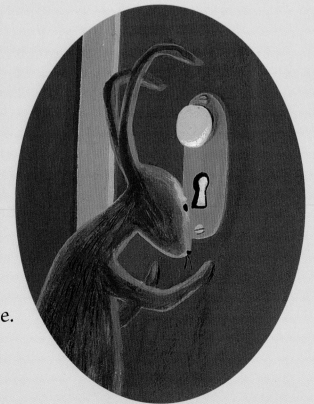

And then suddenly, without even meaning to,
Little Rabbit was looking the night mare in the eye.

"You're not so scary," Little Rabbit
whispered to the night mare. "In fact, you're
not scary at all. Please stop bothering me."

The next day was Friday. Little Rabbit went to school and gave his report about the night mare.

oday is:
Friday
World Map
cupcake
frosting
paper
cake
eat
Sushi!
TALL
Building
Sears Tower

He got a star on his report.

And because he'd finally stopped worrying, Little Rabbit
got a good night's sleep. He dreamed about a different kind
of night mare, one that flew him safely and slowly—and
actually quite comfortably—up to the moon.

"Nice night mare," Little Rabbit said softly in his sleep.
"*Good* night mare."